Ways to [

WE PLAY
DRESS-UP!

By Leonard Atlantic

Gareth Stevens
PUBLISHING

Please visit our website, www.garethstevens.com. For a free color catalog of all our high-quality books, call toll free 1-800-542-2595 or fax 1-877-542-2596.

Cataloging-in-Publication Data

Names: Atlantic, Leonard.
Title: We play dress-up! / Leonard Atlantic.
Description: New York : Gareth Stevens Publishing, 2018. | Series: Ways to play | Includes index.
Identifiers: ISBN 9781482463453 (pbk.) | ISBN 9781482463477 (library bound) | ISBN 9781482463460 (6 pack)
Subjects: LCSH: Children's costumes–Juvenile literature. | Role playing–Juvenile literature
Classification: LCC TT633.A43 2018 | DDC 391–dc23

Published in 2018 by
Gareth Stevens Publishing
111 East 14th Street, Suite 349
New York, NY 10003

Editor: Ryan Nagelhout
Designer: Bethany Perl

Photo credits: Cover, p. 1 (girls) I love photo/Shutterstock.com; p. 1 (background) Photographee.eu/Shutterstock.com; p. 5 Rawpixel.com/Shutterstock.com; p. 7 Angela Waye/Shutterstock.com; pp. 9, 11 Jayme Thornton/The Image Bank/ Getty Images; p. 13 Image Source/Vetta/Getty Images; p. 15 Elena Vasilchenko/Shutterstock.com; p. 17 Becky Wass/Shutterstock.com; p. 19 Sylvie Bouchard/Shutterstock.com; p. 21 Ianych/Shutterstock.com; p. 23 Mat Hayward/Shutterstock.com.

Printed in the United States of America

CPSIA compliance information: Batch #CS17GS: For further information contact Gareth Stevens, New York, New York at 1-800-542-2595.

Contents

My friends love to play with clothes.
This is called dress-up!

We have lots of clothes.
It is fun to try them on.

My brother Dan
looks like a fireman.

He also has a
policeman uniform.

We have funny
hats, too.
One makes me look
like a cowboy!

Lucy likes to wear
a crown.
She is a princess!

We dress up
like animals, too.

My friend Clare looks like a lion!

My friend Cindy is
a bear.

We even dress up
our dog!

Words to Know

cowboy

crown

Index

24